AN AMOROUS
DISCOURSE
IN THE SUBURBS
OF HELL

AN AMOROUS DISCOURSE IN THE SUBURBS OF HELL

Deborah Levy

SHEFFIELD – LONDON – NEW YORK

First published in 1990 by Jonathan Cape, UK

Published with revisions in 2014 by And Other Stories
This edition published in 2023 by And Other Stories
Sheffield – London – New York

www.andotherstories.org

ISBN: 9781913505257
eBook ISBN: 9781908276476

Editors: Sophie Lewis & Stefan Tobler; Copy-editor and Proofreader: Eleanor Crawforth. Typeset in Linotype Swift Neue and Verlag by Tetragon, London. Cover design: Jonathan Pelham. Printed and bound by CPI Limited, Croydon, UK.

A catalogue record for this book is available from the British Library.

And Other Stories gratefully acknowledge that our work is supported using public funding by Arts Council England.

i will not eat tomorrow
and i did not eat today
but wotthehell i ask you
the word is toujours gai

DON MARQUIS,
ARCHY AND MEHITABEL

———

In order to show you where your desire is
it is enough to forbid it to you a little.

a little prohibition
a good deal of play

ROLAND BARTHES,
A LOVER'S DISCOURSE
TRANSLATED BY RICHARD HOWARD

PART ONE

HE

There you are
All wonderful and winged and leaking
That smile
Let me in
Want to
Walk through snow storms
Burning for you
Peeling oranges for you
Shimmering   and
Shivering   my
Assured
Modern
Woman

Who are you
Anyway?

SHE

i have come
to save you
from the suburbs of hell

to rub my skin
against
the regularity of your habits

to bend your thoughts
like a spoon

to find your memories
lost in software

dived like a thought
out of paradise

into
your acrylic arms

HE

Uninvited
You flew into
My semi

And ate all my daffodils

I woke up
To your
Starry tattoos

Fingers
Tangled
In your hair

I asked
You
To stay

Now you make
Incense
From my   heart
And liver

Spit
Mean small
Feathers

At my good intentions

SHE

good intentions
are there
to be ruined

look at the tear stains on your tie

newlyweds
wear a band of gold
full of good intentions

look how they jitter and panic

when the bus stops to change drivers
at the junction between lidl and chicken cottage

HE

No wonder you
Fell
From Grace
Into
My poor lap

Fearful pigeons
Scurry about the roof
Ever since you arrived

SHE

ever since i arrived
on your blue planet
most of it ocean

i hear the breath of an octopus
bigger than a car
eggs in her arms
calling for you

ever since i arrived
i hear the historic echo of yesterday's lambs
under the tarmac of the ring road
baaing and frolicking for you

ever since i arrived
you walk from the table to the window ledge
cursing the pigeons on your roof
their ragged wings
opening and closing for you

HE

How your ragged wings
Open and close
And tell me what to dream

I am my own dreamer
And I'm dreaming of a white Christmas

A little garden
Someone to love
Enough to get by

I can speak French
You can't
I can make shelves

And a wardrobe
With mirrored doors
You can't

If I were more ambitious
I could build a sturdy bridge
But I don't need the acclaim

SHE

yes you can speak french
you read recipe books
as if they were sonnets

yes your wardrobe door
slides on its aluminium runner

yes your shoes have blind eyelets
fastened with coated laces

yet you got hauntings in your eyes
i saw your schoolboy bible
tucked in a corner

you have an uneasy relationship with god
could be interesting

be interesting
be interesting then

spread your hands towards the sky

ask Him in his mercy
to hear your uneasy love

there is no other kind of love
there is no easy kind of love

i don't want provençal dinners from your freezer
i want delirium from under the lake
bang! bang!
watch out stanley
i'm not just unhappy
i'm trigger unhappy
watch the curve of my arm
the sun melt
into the tips
of my fingers

the trees
bending and bowing

HE

Look
I can't afford rhapsody
I was born in Hurstpierpoint
My dad sucks lemon jellies

SHE

then you shouldn't mess about
with an angel
especially one that has been
washed up
on the oil sluck beaches
of yr shores   belly
heaving with the smaller
bellies of fish and birds
find someone sweeter
(unaccustomed to terror)
to laugh at your jokes

HE

Let's get a takeaway. Listen
To the rain
Fill holes.

SHE

suburb man you are cold and unbothered

unlock your front door
the yale and chubb and the chain

take off your shoes
let my wings lift you

to skyscrapers and cornfields
to outraged sons and daughters
to the ferry boat on the 黄浦江
to the currywurst wagon in Friedrichstraße
to the North East SuperFast Express
        (Delhi-Mughal Sarai-Guwahati)

take off your shoes
take off your shoes

dance on a nervous scorpion
dance on the eyelash of a bull
dance on the edge of an oar

unlock your front door
the yale and chubb and the chain

HE

These shoes (size 10, 44 in Europe)
Are for walking in parks, tea
And toast
Afterwards.

Forgive me.
Courage not there.
Sucked by wear and tear
Of 9 to 5 & blocked drains
Eyes are closing.

SHE

die die die of safety
your failing pension plan
a shroud of blind snails
searching for the last green leaf in eden

HE

You are beginning to bore me
Bile and gloom tucked
Tight into your incandescent
Cleavage.   I   would
Rather watch
                    T.V.

SHE

it's true i have these moods.
i might just
      fall
         into
            despair

and singe the carpet
with the heat of my wings
and then
      how
         will you
            console
              me?

i wander around your suburbs in a haze
you fit so well into the seats
of england's expensive trains
i find that when those passengers
who work in financial services
gaze at the back of my head
my garments cease to glisten with light
all my languages desert me
the vibrations of the universe
freeze in the knuckle of my sixth finger

today i will dive under the high-res screen of your
    smart phone
float in the galaxy of samsung
swim through blue tooth and back to ask you

what in essence is an angel?

she is a messenger, mediator, watcher and warner
only trouble is
    desolation
    numbs
    the memory

who was my mother
who was my father
how long have i been falling
is god dead?

am i sick
or have i health?

HE

My health was perfect
Until you fell
On my head   and pressed
Your lips of mist and ice
To mine
You burnt my tongue
You make me nervous
I have a little worldliness
At university
I hennaed my hair
My mother said, only
Whores do that
I wore beads
And had an existential
Girlfriend in a kilt
But now I've grown up
My shirts do not
Scream   and
Beckon   and
        I own
A   water   filter

SHE

worms
worms
worms
in the water
filter or not

there are serpents in paradise
this eden you murdered your discontent to own

oh kiss me quick
i'm fading away
it's all this malice
eating at my   angelic contours
save me . . .

Let me massage you with flower essence
Let me fry you sardines
Let me kiss your cuts and scratches better
Let me plait your saffron hair

Wings stretched East
To West and West to
East, I welcome the
Gift of your arrival

I think I have been
Waiting all my life
To try out the best
Parts of myself

Touch me.

my wings are tinged
with blush
beware
when i weep
there's no stopping
this stuff
pouring
from the circles
of my soul
and i observe
that my cheeks
now itch with bumps
and welts
      i think
         it's
            pollution

PART TWO

HE

I need a woman
To live for
Play the piano to
Cook and have babies with
Share a bed
An address
To measure the sum of my self against

I'm getting on you know
I wake up in the morning
There's a little pile of hair
On the pillow

A deciduous
I'll drop my leaves
For you any day

I am here
In all my shedding glory
For you to
Love.

SHE

you want a woman
to complete
your plan but
it's not my plan

it's not my plan to be completed by you

i keep falling
in and out
of myself

just as i fell out of paradise

i like it that way
sometimes i don't like it that way

for better
or worse
it's the only way

HE

You would destroy my fragile peace
(if you could)
With all the fury of the dispossessed
Look at you hovering above my porcelain egg-cup
You are too big for my possessions
And my possessions are too big for you
Linked as they are to an earthly family tree
I cannot find you on Google, no road no house
No town no country, all you bring to me
Is pain

SHE

discontent is not unattractive
the stage magician who knows nothing of alchemy
and plucks bright balls
from his sleeves   grinning

is far more hideous than you

Discontent is not an achievement
It is not something to win
Like poker or golf or an Oscar

You are suffering
From the absence of
God.

Look how you flap
Your torn wings petulantly
At my modest wallpaper

SHE

i am suffering
from absence point
blank, there's
a hole in my heart
tween you and me
a long-maned horse
could jump through it
with room to spare

HE

Hey, Hey!
Let's let the good times roll
Into the horse-shaped hole in your heart
Listen I'm under the
Influence of your sleazy
Vowels . . . I'm going all funny
And my eyes are shining!

SHE

aw . . .
i love you
like this!

HE

C'mon sweetie
Squeeze into the motor
Let's do 30 when we should do 20
Lets roll over the speed bumps
Let's do that now
While my tank is full
And the price of petrol
Is stable

SHE

just one moment
while i take
this fishbone outta
my teeth.

No. You've lost
The moment. It's
Gone. Stanley is
Himself again.

be someone else
pleeeeeeeeze. just for
the helluvit.

HE

You hurt me
With your desire
For other. I am
Who I am and I
Am fond of myself.

SHE

now you
made me cry with pity
for my poor undone self. all ruffled
and done in

by aristotle's concept of unity.

(384–322 BC)

What do you want
From a human lover?

An
Abstract and
Totally useless
Way of seeing to

    Plunge

        Toes

           Waving

I know you swim at sunrise
With the newts and water voles
In the mud and silt of our Thames
Buffeted by currents and the wash from boats
(I have to blow-dry your wings for hours after)

No one would have you
Wet and melancholy
(You're sort of inconsolable)

Weeping tears of gas
Over the spires of north Ilford

Talk to me straight
Like a motorway
Stay in the left lane
Do not use the hard shoulder
Do not drive against the traffic flow
It's a straight conversation.

SHE

sit here.
Yes here.
that's nice.
straddle my angelic
hips
with yr small town
thighs.

HE

Like this
My sweet feathery
Tormentor?

SHE

it will do.
you ask what i want from a human lover?
i'll tell you straight
like a motorway

a clang! a clamour! a new expression!

That sort of dumbwitted answer
Infuriates the logic
That makes me employable

SHE

it is true
i am a little feverish
soon i will fly to frinton-on-sea
to raise a glass with jane lynne thorburn
    at the three crowns
and then move on to campohermoso
to catch up with francisco rodriguez garrido
trouble is
there are knots in my hair
trouble is
the world is murderously mad

climate maladies, pharmaceuticals
lack of privacy, arms trade possibilities
child marriage in yemen and other tragedies

i will have to look (again)
at aristotle
(384–322 BC)
who i have mentioned
before.
            under his
toga is much to peruse.
if i was to try on his
theory of tragedy
and agree it imitates human acts

i would have to come to the angelic conclusion
that if i was to imitate the acts of human beings

i would have to imitate her not as she is

but as she could be

HE

Erm . . . I find your
Angelic hips alienating.
You thrash about in some bedlam
For the winged and divine
Forgetting you have a mortal
On your knee. My moustache is
Full of froth. I don't understand
Say again what you said?

SHE

i said nothing
i said nothing
i said looking

        down into the suburbs
and beyond
i saw
sad stars   fall
like halos
on men and women
howling into the damp crease of their past

i saw first worlds
blister   the skin
of other worlds

zebras
gallop   through
burning suns   to
the shade of long
grasses,   and

somewhere else,   love
affairs in old hotels
with balconies

i saw beggars beg
in every language   children fear
death in every language

and i saw you
weeping on your doormat
decided to   become
a commuter
between heaven
and
the suburbs of hell

you seemed like a good
sort of man
an accountant
with culinary tendencies
tho' lacking in charisma
(look at your tie)
the task
to
bring you
into
the light
and dark
of uncertainty

the two great themes
of classical science

chaos
      and
           order

undressing and
dressing and
cross dressing and
overdressing and
addressing envelopes

HE

Sounds like hard work
To me
I like plain shampoos
Soaps
Ecologically sound
Detergents
One hundred per cent
Wool
Good strong tea
Olive oil (budget permitting)
I like the light
To be just light
And the dark
To just be dark
I do not wish to live in a grey area
Or to read between the lines
Love must start on the first line
Continue on every line
No line without love
And then she marries me
That is my wish

SHE

get off my knee
stanley . . .
now!
i try to introduce you
to the way i see things
and all you want is a wife
a wife and a second-class stamp and a bath
a bath and a donut and a product to kill moths

HE

You're just a totalitarian angel
Full of self-rapture
I thought you were a divine messenger
In fact you're a glutton
With wings

SHE

you are suburbia's satisfied son

i came to you
naked
glittering

flew through a chernobyl storm

above the pripyat river and its seven left tributaries
pina, yaselda, tsna, lan, sluch, ptsich, braginka

to find your microwave dreaming of you

yes dreaming of you
kneeling in a nuclear forest
gathering mushrooms in lithuania

pinging
pinging
pinging

dreaming in stainless steel for you

HE

You came to me
At the moment
I did battle with my soul
And found myself
Weeping on the doormat

Journeyed through
The storm in my heart
To heal the wounded

And yet the healer
Is more wounded than myself.

Your discontent
Has shattered
My double glazing
Twice

Who taught you
To behave like that?

This is a gentle place
With ancient trees
And often blossom

Go away
And don't come back
Fuck off
Out of my easily
Satisfied arms.

SHE

so cruel you are
secretly. untangle
this bird caught
in my hair. it blew
in from somewhere
made me yearn
for hugs and
boat rides

i've got all plump
from lack of euphoria.

HE

Ha!
Despite your sizzling proclamations
I am happier than you

Though you despise me for it

I listen to the weather forecast

Enjoy peaceful walks
In appropriate clothing

Sleep well at night

Do I need you?

Though flattered to be visited by an angel
With a mission
I prefer talking to my postman
His name is Shivadhar
In winter he wears a black beanie
With a bobble and I want one
In blue.

Tonight
I will eat
Pad Thai and drink
Singha beer
With my brother
Grateful

For small pleasures
We can share

All the while
Glad to be sure
The sun will always set in the West

And dusk settle over this suburb of bankrupt councils
Retail click-and-collect centres
Mental health tribunals

And me
And Shivadhar
And my brother.

Did you say you can hear a frog
Splashing at the end of the world?

SHE

i said nothing
i said something
i said never talk to the hand

when you have an angel
perched on your wrist

you are a human subject
living and furious

architect of your own paradise
on this grave earth

of splendid contraries

it's been a pleasure
to know you
and then know
you a little bit more

                   fry me a sardine
              the wind is blowing
                  i'll be off.

Dear readers,

As well as relying on bookshop sales, And Other Stories relies on subscriptions from people like you for many of our books, whose stories other publishers often consider too risky to take on.

Our subscribers don't just make the books physically happen. They also help us approach booksellers, because we can demonstrate that our books already have readers and fans. And they give us the security to publish in line with our values, which are collaborative, imaginative and 'shamelessly literary'.

All of our subscribers:

- receive a first-edition copy of each of the books they subscribe to
- are thanked by name at the end of our subscriber-supported books
- receive little extras from us by way of thank you, for example: postcards created by our authors

BECOME A SUBSCRIBER, OR GIVE A SUBSCRIPTION TO A FRIEND

Visit andotherstories.org/subscriptions to help make our books happen. You can subscribe to books we're in the process of making. To purchase books we have already published, we urge you to support your local or favourite bookshop and order directly from them – the often unsung heroes of publishing.

OTHER WAYS TO GET INVOLVED

If you'd like to know about upcoming events and reading groups (our foreign-language reading groups help us choose books to publish, for example) you can:

- join our mailing list at: andotherstories.org
- follow us on Twitter: @andothertweets
- join us on Facebook: facebook.com/AndOtherStoriesBooks
- admire our books on Instagram: @andotherpics
- follow our blog: andotherstories.org/ampersand

This book was made possible thanks to the support of:

Adam Butler
Adam Lenson
Adrian May
AG Hughes
Aidan Cottrell-Boyce
Aine Bourke
Ajay Sharma
Alan Ramsey
Alannah Hopkin
Alastair Dickson
Alastair Gillespie
Alastair Laing
Alec Begley
Alex Martin
Alex Ramsey
Alex Sutcliffe
Alexandra Buchler
Alexandra de Verseg-
   Roesch
Ali Conway
Ali Smith
Alice Nightingale
Alisa Brookes
Alison Hughes
Alison Winston
Allison Graham
Alyse Ceirante
Amanda Anderson
Amanda Banham
Amanda Dalton
Amanda Love Darragh
Amelia Ashton
Amelia Dowe
Amy Rushton
Amy Webster
Ana Amália Alves
Andrea Davis
Andrew Marston
Andrew McCafferty
Andrew Nairn

Andrew Pattison
Andy Burfield
Andy Paterson
Angela Thirlwell
Angharad Eyre
Angus MacDonald
Angus Walker
Ann McAllister
Ann Van Dyck
Anna Milsom
Anna Vinegrad
Anna-Karin Palm
Annabel Hagg
Annalise Pippard
Anne Carus
Anne Claydon-Wallace
Anne Maguire
Anne Waugh
Anne Clair Le Reste
Anne Marie Jackson
Annette Nugent
Annie McDermott
Anonymous
Antonio de Swift
Antony Pearce
Archie Davies
Asher Norris
Averill Buchanan
Ayca Turkoglu
Barbara Latham
Barbara Mellor
Barbara Thanni
Barbara Zybutz
Barry Norton
Bartolomie Tyszka
Belinda Farrell
Ben Paynter
Ben Schofield
Ben Smith
Ben Thornton

Benjamin Judge
Benjamin Morris
Blanka Stoltz
Bob Hill
Brenda Scott
Brendan McIntyre
Briallen Hopper
Bruce Ackers
Bruce Millar
Bruce & Maggie
   Holmes
C Baker
C Mieville
Calum Colley
Candy Says Juju
   Sophie
Cara & Bali Haque
Carole JS Russo
Caroline Adie
Caroline Perry
Caroline Rigby
Carolyn A Schroeder
Cath Drummond
Cecily Maude
Charles Lambert
Charles Rowley
Charlotte Baines
Charlotte Holtam
Charlotte Ryland
Charlotte Whittle
Chris Day
Chris Hancox
Chris Radley
Chris Stevenson
Chris Wood
Chris Elcock
Christina Baum
Christina
   MacSweeney
Christina Scholz

Christine Lovell
Christine Luker
Christopher Allen
Christopher Marlow
Ciara Ní Riain
Ciarán Oman
Claire Fuller
Claire Mitchell
Claire Tranah
Clare Fisher
Clare Keates
Clare Lucas
Clarissa Botsford
Claudio Guerri
Clifford Posner
Clive Bellingham
Colin Burrow
Collette Eales
Courtney Lilly
Craig Barney
Dan Pope
Daniel Carpenter
Daniel Gillespie
Daniel Hahn
Daniel Hugill
Daniel Lipscombe
Daniel Sheldrake
Daniel Venn
Daniel James Fraser
Daniela Steierberg
Dave Lander
David Archer
David Breuer
David Eales
David Gould
David Hedges
David Higgins
David Johnson-Davies
David Roberts
David Smith
Dawn Mazarakis
Debbie Pinfold

Deborah Bygrave
Deborah Jacob
Deborah Smith
Delia Cowley
Denise Jones
Denise Muir
Denise Sewell
Diana Brighouse
DW Wilson & A
    Howard
Eddie Dick
Edward Baggs
Eileen Buttle
EJ Baker
Elaine Martel
Elaine Rassaby
Eleanor Maier
Elina Zicmane
Eliza O'Toole
Elizabeth Draper
Elizabeth Polonsky
Emily Jeremiah
Emily Taylor
Emily Williams
Emily Yaewon Lee &
    Gregory Limpens
Emma Bielecki
Emma Kenneally
Emma Teale
Emma Timpany
Eva Tobler-Zumstein
Evgenia Loginova
Ewan Tant
Fawzia Kane
Ferdinand Craig Hall
Fi McMillan
Fiona Doepel
Fiona Graham
Fiona Powlett Smith
Fiona Quinn
Florian Andrews
Fran Sanderson

Frances Chapman
Francesca Bray
Francis Taylor
Francisco Vilhena
Freya Carr
G Thrower
Gale Pryor
Garry Wilson
Gavin Collins
Gawain Espley
Gemma Tipton
Genevra Richardson
Geoffrey Fletcher
George McCaig
George Savona
George Wilkinson
George Sandison &
    Daniela Laterza
Georgia Panteli
Geraldine Brodie
Gill Boag-Munroe
Gillian Doherty
Gillian Jondorf
Gillian Spencer
Gillian Stern
Giselle Maynard
Gloria Sully
Glyn Ridgley
Gordon Cameron
Gordon Campbell
Gordon Mackechnie
Graham Hardwick
Graham & Steph
    Parslow
Graham R Foster
Gwyn Wallace
Hannah Perret
Hanne Larsson
Hannes Heise
Harriet Gamper
Harriet Mossop
Harriet Owles

Harriet Sayer
Harriet Spencer
Helen Asquith
Helen Bailey
Helen Buck
Helen Collins
Helen Weir
Helen Wormald
Helen Brady
Helena Taylor
Helene Walters
Henrike Laehnemann
Howdy Reisdorf
Hugh Buckingham
Ian Barnett
Ian Kirkwood
Ian McMillan
Irene Mansfield
Isabel Costello
Isabella Garment
Isobel Staniland
J Collins
Jack Brown
Jacky Oughton
Jacqueline Crooks
Jacqueline Haskell
Jacqueline Taylor
Jacqueline Lademann
Jacqueline & Alistair
    Douglas
Jacquie Goacher
Jade Maitre
James Clark
James Cubbon
James Huddie
James Portlock
James Scudamore
James Tierney
James Upton
James & Mapi
Jane Brandon
Jane Whiteley

Jane Woollard
Janet Bolam
Janet Mullarney
Janette Ryan
Jasmine Dee Cooper
Jasmine Gideon
Jason Spencer
JC Sutcliffe
Jeff Collins
Jen Grainger
Jen Hamilton-Emery
Jenifer Logie
Jennifer Higgins
Jennifer Hurstfield
Jennifer O'Brien
Jennifer Watson
Jenny Diski
Jenny Newton
Jeremy Weinstock
Jerry Lynch
Jess Wood
Jethro Soutar
Jillian Jones
Jim Boucherat
Jo Elvery
Jo Harding
Jo Hope
Joan Clinch
Joanne Hart
Jocelyn English
Jodie Free
Joel Love
Johan Forsell
Johannes Georg Zipp
John Allison
John Conway
John Fisher
John Gent
John Hodgson
John Kelly
John Nicholson
John Steph Grainger

Jon Gower
Jon Iglesias
Jon Lindsay Miles
Jonathan Evans
Jonathan Watkiss
Joseph Cooney
Josephine Burton &
    Jeremy Gordon
JP Sanders
Judith Heneghan
Judith Norton
Judy Kendall
Julian Duplain
Julian Lomas
Juliane Jarke
Julie Freeborn
Julie Gibson
Julie Van Pelt
Kaarina Hollo
Kaitlin Olson
Kalbinder Dayal
Kapka Kassabova
Karan Deep Singh
Kari Dickson
Karla Fonesca
Katarina Trodden
Kate Gardner
Kate Griffin
Kate Rhind
Kate Waugh
Katharina Liehr
Katharine Freeman
Katharine Robbins
Katherine Jacomb
Kathryn Lewis
Katia Leloutre
Katie Smith
Kay Elmy
Keith Alldritt
Keith Dunnett
Ken Walsh
Kevin Acott

Kevin Brockmeier
Kevin Pino
KL Ee
Koen Van Bockstal
Kristin Djuve
Krystalli Glyniadakis
Lana Selby
Larry Colbeck
Laura Bennett
Laura Clarke
Laura Jenkins
Laura Solon
Laura Woods
Lauren Ellemore
Lauren Kassell
Leanne Bass
Leonie Schwab
Lesley Lawn
Lesley Murphey
Lesley Watters
Leslie Leuck
Leslie Rose
Linda Harte
Lindsay Brammer
Lindsey Ford
Liz Clifford
Liz Tunnicliffe
Loretta Platts
Lorna Bleach
Louise Bongiovanni
Louise Rogers
Louise S Smith
Lucie Donahue
Lucie Harris
Lucy Luke
Lynda Graham
Lynn Martin
M Manfre
Madeleine Kleinwort
Maeve Lambe
Maggie Peel
Maisie & Nick Carter

Malcolm Bourne
Marella Oppenheim
Mareta & Conor Doyle
Margaret Jull Costa
Maria Pelletta
Marina Castledine
Marina Lomunno
Marion Cole
Marion England
Marion Tricoire
Mark Ainsbury
Mark Howdle
Mark Stevenson
Mark Waters
Marta Muntasell
Martha Gifford
Martha Nicholson
Martin Brampton
Martin Hollywood
Mary Hall
Mary Wang
Mary Ann Horgan
Matt Oldfield
Matt Riggott
Matthew Bates
Matthew Francis
Matthew Lawrence
Matthew Steventon
Matthew Todd
Maureen Freely
Maxime Dargaud-Fons
Melissa da Silveira
   Serpa
Michael Harrison
Michael Johnston
Michael Kitto
Michael & Christine
   Thompson
Michelle Bailat-Jones
Michelle Roberts
Miles Visman
Milo Waterfield

Monika Olsen
Morgan Lyons
Moshi Moshi Records
Murali Menon
N Jabinh
Nan Craig
Nan Haberman
Nasser Hashmi
Natalie Smith
Natalie Wardle
Natasha
   Soobramanien
Nathalie Adams
Nathaniel Barber
Nia Emlyn-Jones
Nicci Rodie
Nick Judd
Nick Williams
Nick James
Nick Nelson & Rachel
   Eley
Nicola Balkind
Nicola Hart
Nicola Hughes
Nina Alexandersen
Noah Birksted-Breen
Nora Gombos
Nuala Watt
Owen Booth
Pamela Ritchie
Pat Crowe
Patrick Owen
Paul Bailey
Paul Brand
Paul Hannon
Paul Hollands
Paul Jones
Paul Miller
Paul Munday
Paul Myatt
Paul Sullivan
Paul M Cray

Paula McGrath
Penelope Price
Peter Armstrong
Peter Burns
Peter Law
Peter Lawton
Peter Murray
Peter Rowland
Peter Vos
Philip Warren
Philippe Royer
Phyllis Reeve
Piet Van Bockstal
Pipa Clements
PM Goodman
Polly McLean
Rachael Williams
Rachel Bailey
Rachel Henderson
Rachel Kennedy
Rachel Lasserson
Rachel Van Riel
Rachel Watkins
Read MAW Books
Rebecca Atkinson
Rebecca Braun
Rebecca Moss
Rebecca Rosenthal
Renata Larkin
Rhian Jones
Rhodri Jones
Richard Ellis
Richard Jackson
Richard Smith
Richard Wales
Rishi Dastidar
Rob Jefferson-Brown
Robert Gillett
Robert Saunders
Robin Patterson
Robin Woodburn
Rodolfo Barradas

Rory Sullivan
Ros Schwartz
Rose Cole
Rose Skelton
Rosemary Rodwell
Ross Macpherson
Rossana
Roz Simpson
Russell Logan
Ruth Stokes
Ruth F Hunt
SE Guine
SJ Bradley
SJ Naudé
Sabine Griffiths
Sally Baker
Sam Ruddock
Samantha Sabbarton-
    Wright
Sandra de Monte
Sandra Hall
Sandy Derbyshire
Sara D'Arcy
Sarah Benson
Sarah Butler
Sarah Duguid
Sarah Fakray
Sarah Pybus
Sarah Salmon
Sarah Salway
Sasha Dugdale
Saskia Restorick
Sean Malone
Sean McGivern
Sharon Evans
Shazea Quraishi
Sheridan Marshall
Sherine El-Sayed
Shirley Harwood
Sigrun Hodne
Simon Armstrong
Simon Pare

Simon Pennington
Simon Thomson
Simon John Harvey
Simona Constantin
Sinead Rippington
Siobhan Higgins
Sonia McLintock
Sophie Eustace
Sophie North
Stef Kennedy
Stefano D'Orilia
Steph Morris
Stephanie Brada
Stephen Abbott
Stephen Pearsall
Stephen Walker
Stephen H Oakey
Stewart McAbney
Stuart Condie
Sue Doyle
Sue & Ed Aldred
Sunil Samani
Susan Tomaselli
Susie Roberson
Suzanne White
Tammy Watchorn
Tamsin Ballard
Tania Hershman
Tasmin Maitland
Thomas Bell
Thomas Fritz
Thomas JD Gray
Tien Do
Tim Gray
Tim Jackson
Tim Robins
Tim Theroux
Tim Warren
Timothy Harris
Tina Rotherham-
    Winqvist
Todd Greenwood

Tom Bowden
Tom Darby
Tom Franklin
Tony Messenger
Tony Roa
Tony & Joy Molyneaux
Torna Russell-Hills
Tracey Martin
Tracy Northup
Trevor Lewis

Trevor Wald
Trilby Humphryes
Tristan Burke
Val Challen
Vanessa Garden
Vanessa Nolan
Vasco Dones
Venetia Welby
Victoria Adams
Victoria Walker

Visaly Muthusamy
Viviane D'Souza
Walter Prando
Wendy Irvine
Wendy Langridge
Wendy Toole
Wenna Price
William G Dennehy
Yukiko Hiranuma
Zoe Brasier

CURRENT & UPCOMING BOOKS

DEBORAH LEVY is a British playwright, novelist and poet. Her novels include the Booker-shortlisted *Swimming Home* (2011) and *Hot Milk* (2016), and the Booker-longlisted *The Man Who Saw Everything* (2019).

Deborah is also the author of a collection of short stories, *Black Vodka* (2013), and a trilogy of prize-winning Living Autobiographies: *Things I Don't Want to Know*, *The Cost of Living*, and *Real Estate*.

She has written for the Royal Shakespeare Company and the BBC. *An Amorous Discourse in the Suburbs of Hell* was first published in 1990 by Jonathan Cape and appears now in a new and revised edition.